Dinosaur School

NEAR AND FAR

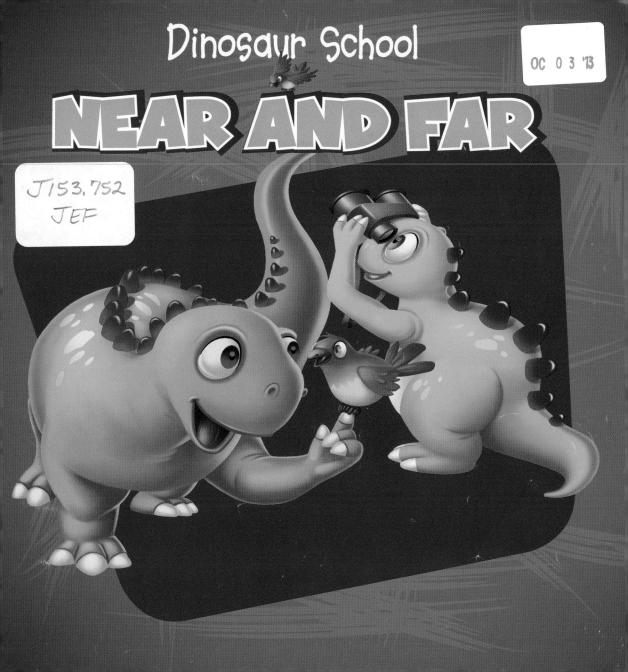

Please visit our website, www.garethstevens.com. For a free color catalog of all our high-quality books, call toll free 1-800-542-2595 or fax 1-877-542-2596.

Library of Congress Cataloging-in-Publication Data

Jeffries, Joyce.
 Near and far / Joyce Jeffries.
     p. cm. — (Dinosaur school)
 ISBN 978-1-4339-8100-5 (pbk.)
 ISBN 978-1-4339-8101-2 (6-pack)
 ISBN 978-1-4339-8099-2 (library binding)
 1. Depth perception—Juvenile literature. I. Title.
 BF469.J44 2013
 153.7'52—dc23

                                    2012034598

First Edition

Published in 2013 by
Gareth Stevens Publishing
111 East 14th Street, Suite 349
New York, NY 10003

Copyright © 2013 Gareth Stevens Publishing

Designer: Mickey Harmon
Editor: Katie Kawa

All illustrations by Planman Technologies

Printed in the United States of America

CPSIA compliance information: Batch #CW13GS: For further information contact Gareth Stevens, New York, New York at 1-800-542-2595.

NEAR AND FAR

By Joyce Jeffries

Gareth Stevens
Publishing

The dog is near.

The dog is far.

The car is near.

The car is far.

The house is near.

The house is far.

The bird is near.

The bird is far.

The balloon is near.

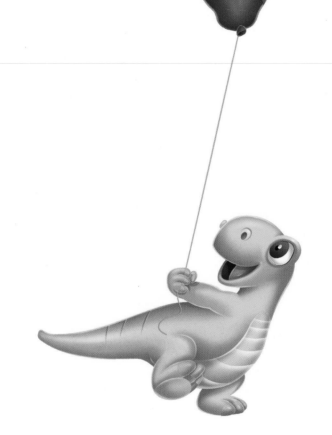

The balloon is far.

The cat is near.

The cat is far.

The ball is near.

The ball is far.

The box is near.

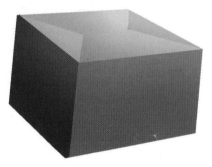

The box is far.

The horse is near.

The horse is far.

The train is near.

The train is far.

Near and Far

FAR

NEAR

24